Rosa's Big Sunflower Experiment

Yap!
Yap!

Child's Play (International) Ltd
Ashworth Rd, Bridgemead, Swindon SN5 7YD, UK
Swindon   Auburn ME   Sydney
ISBN 978-1-78628-364-1   WP281119CBB03203641
© 2020 Child's Play (International) Ltd
Printed in Guangdong, China
1 3 5 7 9 10 8 6 4 2
www.childs-play.com

Rosa and her friends want to plant sunflower seeds.
"Fill each pot with soil," says Rosa.

"Tweezers are best for collecting seeds from this dried sunflower," says Misha. Shala laughs, "They look huge through my magnifying glass!"

"Sunflower begins with an S," explains Rosa.

"What does 'germinate' mean?"
asks Shala.
Dawson looks in a book.
"I think it's when a seedling
begins to grow," he says.

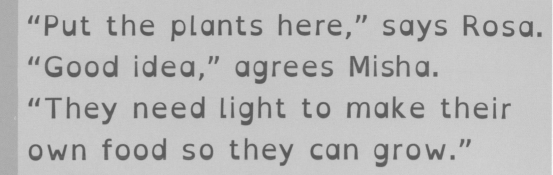

"Put the plants here," says Rosa.
"Good idea," agrees Misha.
"They need light to make their
own food so they can grow."

"How long will it take for our seeds to flower?" asks Dawson.
"About 80 days," replies Rosa.

"Wow! These plants are really growing fast," says Dawson.

"I left this one in the dark," sighs Shala. "You can see what happens with no light or water."

"Oh no, Snowy Dog!" exclaims Rosa.
"Wow!" says Misha.
"Look at all those roots."

sunflower

"Roots support the plant," explains Misha.
"They suck up the water and nutrients from the soil."
"I think this one is dead," sighs Rosa.

"Good digging, Snowy Dog!" laughs Rosa. "Planting the sunflowers out here will really help them grow big."

"Look at the height of those!" shouts Rosa. "Growing plants is great for all the minibeasts!"

flower

stem

leaf